MYSTERIES
OF THE
OVERWORLD

MYSTERIES OF THE OVERWORLD

AN UNOFFICIAL OVERWORLD HEROES ADVENTURE, BOOK TWO

DANICA DAVIDSON

Sky Pony Press
New York

Copyright © 2018 by Danica Davidson

Minecraft® is a registered trademark of Notch Development AB.

The Minecraft game is copyright © Mojang AB.

This book is not authorized or sponsored by Microsoft Corp., Mojang AB,
Notch Development AB or Scholastic Inc., or any other person or entity
owning or controlling rights in the Minecraft name, trademark, or copyrights.

All rights reserved. No part of this book may be reproduced in any manner
without the express written consent of the publisher, except in the case of
brief excerpts in critical reviews or articles. All inquiries should be addressed
to Sky Pony Press, 307 West 36th Street, 11th Floor, New York, NY 10018.

Sky Pony Press books may be purchased in bulk at special discounts for sales
promotion, corporate gifts, fund-raising, or educational purposes. Special
editions can also be created to specifications. For details, contact the Special
Sales Department, Sky Pony Press, 307 West 36th Street, 11th Floor,
New York, NY 10018 or info@skyhorsepublishing.com.

Sky Pony® is a registered trademark of Skyhorse Publishing, Inc.®,
a Delaware corporation.

Minecraft® is a registered trademark of Notch Development AB.
The Minecraft game is copyright © Mojang AB.

Visit our website at www.skyponypress.com.

10 9 8 7 6 5 4 3 2 1

Library of Congress Cataloging-in-Publication Data is available on file.

Cover design by Brian Peterson
Cover photo by Lordwhitebear

Paperback ISBN: 978-1-5107-2703-8
Ebook ISBN: 978-1-5107-2709-0

Printed in Canada

MYSTERIES
OF THE
OVERWORLD

CHAPTER 1

MY COUSIN ALEX WAS POUNDING ON THE front door so hard you'd think every monster in the Overworld was chasing her. As soon as I opened the door, she rushed inside the house, her eyes wild. She gasped, "I found something that changes everything! You have to come see! Right now!"

"Is this about the crystal shard?" I asked.

Just days before, Alex, my friends from Earth, and I had fought off an army of Endermen to protect a strange, purple crystal shard we'd found. We'd figured out the crystal shard possessed some kind of very old magic and the Endermen wanted to use it so they could release somebody—or *something*—extremely dangerous from some kind of prison. Some people who'd touched the crystal, including me, had even heard an evil woman's voice in our heads. But we still had no idea exactly what the crystal was, or what it could do.

"I said, let's *go*!" Alex demanded, not bothering to answer me. She was still catching her breath from running.

"Dad, I'm going out with Alex!" I called as Alex grabbed me by my turquoise shirt and yanked me out of the house. Dad's reminder to be careful was cut off by the door closing.

My cousin tended to be as fiery as her red hair, but this was wild even for her. She must have found something big.

"I was searching the area, trying to find clues about the crystal," Alex said as she ran, "and I discovered some old mineshafts near where you found the shard."

Alex wanted to be an explorer when she grew up, and she already explored her heart out whenever she got the chance.

"Stevie," Alex said, panting. "Get ready to have everything you know about the Overworld turned upside down."

"What do you mean?" I said, rushing to keep up with her. My pulse was pounding in my ears, and it wasn't just from running.

She shook her head. "It's something you just have to see."

A recent Wither attack had opened up a crevice in a mountain, and Alex led me to the far side of the blast.

There was a hole in the ground and Alex leapt down into it, shouting, "Follow me!"

I didn't have any weapons with me, and I knew monsters—also called mobs—could be lurking in that dark mineshaft. But Alex did have her arrows, and I needed to see what she was so excited about. If it solved the crystal shard mystery and stopped the creepy voice . . .

Get me out of this prison. I'm ready to rule again, the voice had said to my friend Maison. The voice was so malicious that remembering it gave me the heebie-jee-bies even now. I took a deep breath and followed Alex down into the darkness.

In the mineshaft Alex pulled out a torch to give us a little light. "Look at this," she said.

We'd come up to a door. In the torchlight I could see it was etched with the same fancy symbols I'd found on the door that led to the crystal shard. It looked like a fancy S and A looped together like a design.

My heart leapt into my throat. There might be some really good clues in there.

Alex opened the door with a nearby switch.

"Did you find another crystal shard?" I asked.

She said, "No, even better."

We crept into the room. It was ghostly silent, like it held the silence of the centuries that it had been abandoned and untouched. Our footfalls were as loud as thunder.

"Look at this," Alex said, picking up a book and handing it to me.

The book was dusty, but I could see someone had already smeared some of the dust off the cover so they could read it. That must have been Alex earlier. The cover had the same S and A design on it in golden letters.

I started to open the book, but the pages wouldn't budge for some reason.

"I couldn't get it open, either," Alex said. "It must need a key, but I haven't found any around here. But look—turn it over."

I flipped the book over. On the back was a drawing of a purple crystal shard. "This looks just like the shard we found!" I said.

Alex nodded. "Imagine what we could find inside," she said. "It might explain all the mysterious things that have been going on"

I was getting excited. "Maybe my dad will know how to open it," I said. My dad knew just about everything about the Overworld, though the crystal shard had stumped him. We were keeping it safely hidden away in our house, and he had been visiting libraries in nearby villages to search for information and ask the villagers about it. So far all the librarians were clueless.

"That's not even the most mind-blowing part," Alex said. "Look."

She took me over to the mineshaft wall, moving the torch close so I could see. Someone had carved an image in the wall of a strong-looking man standing in a heroic way, holding up his diamond sword. It looked like he was daring mobs to attack him—as though he knew he could take anyone on.

"It's just Steve Alexander," I said, feeling let down. I thought Alex was going to show me something more impressive than this after all that you-just-have-to-see-it-for-yourself-Stevie talk. Steve Alexander had lived thousands of years ago, and he had become a legend. Everyone knew who he was, and lots of people in the Overworld named their kids Steve, Alexander, Stephanie, and Alexandra because of him. My name was Stevie, and my dad's name was Steve, and his dad's name was Steve, and his dad's—well, I think you get the point.

It was the same for my cousin. Alex was a nickname for Alexandra. Her mom was named Alexandra, and all the firstborn daughters in the family had been given the same name for generations.

So there were images of Steve Alexander everywhere. In the nearby village there was a big statue of him in the same pose, holding up his diamond sword. Dad and Aunt Alexandra had always said that Alex and I were descendants of Steve Alexander, but everyone told their kids that. When I was little, Alex and I sometimes argued with other kids over who was really related to Steve Alexander. That's how I realized all the kids had been told the same thing. So I stopped believing it, though Alex was still convinced we were related to him.

And who wouldn't want to be related to someone so heroic? Before Steve Alexander had come along, the world had been so overrun with mobs that people had to hide in their homes all the time. We still had to deal with mobs these days, but things were much better now because of him.

"I'm not talking about Steve Alexander," Alex said. "Look. You can tell this image is really old, right?"

"Yeah," I said. You could see from the way it was carved that it had been on the wall for centuries, at least. It might have even been made when Steve Alexander was still alive.

Alex moved the torchlight to the side. Next to the familiar image of Steve Alexander was an image of a woman carved into the rock.

This time my heart jumped so high in my throat I almost choked on it.

"This can't be," I said. I grabbed the torch from Alex's hand to hold it closer, convinced I was seeing the image wrong. I wasn't. My eyes were absolutely, positively not playing tricks on me.

This image looked as old as the Steve Alexander carving, and you could tell by the way they were carved next to each other that they were connected.

The carved woman had an emerald-shaped face, long, thick hair, and wise eyes. She was standing with her arms crossed in front of her stomach, her long fingers touching her arms.

No one in the Overworld had her body shape. No one in the Overworld had fingers.

This was a woman from Earth.

CHAPTER 2

"**B**UT I THOUGHT NO ONE IN THE OVERWORLD knew about Earth until I discovered the portal," I said.

"That's what I thought too," Alex said. "Now you see why I had to show it to you?"

Earlier that year I'd accidentally found a strange-looking portal, and when I went through it, it hadn't led to the Nether or the End. Instead I'd fallen out of a computer screen and into a realm called Earth, where people had fingers and cell phones, and the spiders were tiny instead of big and red-eyed. It was there that I'd met my friends Maison, Destiny, and Yancy, who'd helped me save the Overworld many times since. They'd also been part of the battle against the Enderman army to protect the crystal shard.

No one I knew in the Overworld had ever seen Earth people before I introduced them to my friends. Was it possible someone from Earth had been here before? Or . . . had Steve Alexander been to Earth? There were a ton of legends about Steve Alexander, including the legend that he discovered the End. But there was no legend about him discovering Earth.

"I told you this changes everything," Alex rattled on. I still couldn't say anything. "If we had contact between the worlds that far back . . ."

"We need to tell my dad," I blurted. "And we need to get Maison and the others."

A short while later, Dad, Alex, Maison, Destiny, Yancy, and I sat at my kitchen table, staring at the mysterious book. We'd just returned from another trip to the mineshaft to show everyone the images carved on the wall. I'd told Maison that I thought the woman looked a little bit like her and she had said, "I hope I'm as wise as she is when I'm older." So I wasn't the only one who thought the woman looked very wise.

"Maybe the 'S A' stands for Steve Alexander," Maison said as she tried to open the book. It wouldn't budge for her, either.

"Who is this Steve Alexander?" Yancy said. "I'm a big *Minecraft* fan, but I've never heard of him."

"He's the biggest hero the Overworld has ever had," Alex said. "And we're related to him."

"Alex, everyone says that," I said. "He lived too long ago for anyone to trace their family all the way back to him."

Dad put his hand to his square beard, thinking. Then, without a word, he walked out to the supply shed.

I turned back to the book. Destiny was squinting at it and frowning.

"Destiny, put your glasses on," Yancy said.

Destiny made a face and pulled something out of her pocket. It looked like two pieces of glass in a frame. She set them over her nose.

"Destiny, I didn't know you wore glasses," Maison said.

"I just got them recently," Destiny said, frowning. "Some of the other kids made fun of me."

"They help you see," Maison said, sounding angry. "Why would anyone make fun of you for that?"

I'd seen other people in Maison's world wear glasses, but this was the first time I'd seen them up close. "How do they work?" I asked, curious. "Do you enchant the glass?"

Then I realized I probably sounded silly. On Earth, there was no such thing as enchantment.

"No, they just cut glass to help you see. Look." Destiny put the glasses in front of my face, but all the glass did was make my vision blurry.

"Whoa," I said, pushing the glasses away. They made me dizzy. "I think those are broken."

"They work for my eyes," Destiny said. "Everyone who needs glasses needs a different prescription."

Earth's weird ways were usually pretty interesting to me, but right then I mainly wanted to figure out what the book was and why there was an Earth woman's image on that wall. I handed Destiny her glasses back just as Dad walked back into the kitchen. He was holding a key with the same S-A symbolism on it.

"Where did you get that?" I exclaimed.

Was there a slight trace of a smile on Dad's face? "This is a family heirloom that's been passed down from Steve to Steve for generations. It originally belonged to Steve Alexander, your ancestor."

I guessed Dad hadn't liked me scoffing Steve Alexander earlier. But this was a shock! So . . . did that mean I really *was* Steve Alexander's descendant?

Dad put the key into the book's little keyhole. And just like that, the book swung open.

CHAPTER 3

"WHAT IS THIS, GIBBERISH?" ALEX COMplained. The book was filled with squiggly lines, like someone mimicking what writing should look like.

"In the *Minecraft* game, books can look like this," Yancy said.

"Yeah, in your *game*," Alex said bitterly. "In our world, we can read books. This is—this is just nothing!" She slapped the book to the floor.

Maison picked the book back up and began flipping the pages. It was all filled with the same weird writing.

"Is there some way to enchant this to let us read it?" she asked.

"I don't do enchantments," Dad said. "Never cared much for it. But maybe the village librarian will know something about this."

"We'll take it to the village," I said, ready to head out the door.

But Dad stopped me. "No," he said. "This book is probably valuable. It needs to stay where it's safe, and this house is protected. I'll bring the librarian back here to take a look."

"Is it all right if we stay here and keep trying to find ways to read it?" Maison said.

Dad shrugged. "I don't see any harm in it. You kids stay here and I'll be back."

He picked up his toolkit and walked out the door. The rest of us bent back over the book.

Alex took the book and shook it. "Why won't you work, you stupid thing?"

"Relax, Alex," Yancy said. "It's not an Etch A Sketch."

"A *what*?" Alex said.

Yancy gently took the book from her and looked at the image on the back. "It's about the same size as the crystal shard," he mused. "I wonder if that means anything. Where are you keeping that shard, Stevie?"

"I'll go get it," I said.

We were storing it in a little box made of iron that Dad and I had made in an attempt to keep it extra safe. No one had bothered us since the Enderman army the other day, but we had a feeling that someone would come for the crystal shard eventually. Since Endermen didn't like water, Dad had also put a water source block on top of the house to fend them off. That meant water was constantly drizzling down our roof, and we had to be careful not to get wet when we went in and out of the house. But it was a small price to pay to know the shard was safe.

I opened the iron box and hesitated. I really hated holding the crystal—I never knew when I would hear that awful voice. I made myself pick it up. The crystal glowed violet in my palm, but I didn't hear any voices. Phew.

Yancy set the book down on the table with the back cover facing up. I put the crystal on top of the drawing, and it was the perfect fit, almost like someone had traced it to get the design on the book.

"Interesting," Yancy said, picking the crystal up while Maison opened the book back up and squinted at it. "Stevie," Yancy went on, "I know your dad's not into enchantments, but I like to do them when I play *Minecraft*, and . . ."

Suddenly, Yancy's whole body tensed like he was in pain. He uttered a low cry and dropped the crystal, letting it fall on the open front page of the book.

I watched in horror as Yancy grabbed his black hair between his long, pale fingers. It was like he was trying to rip something out of his brain. I already knew what must have happened.

"Did you hear a voice?" Maison said, her head snapping up. She and I had both experienced it before.

Yancy shuddered. "That wasn't just any voice," he said. "That was a . . . a nightmare! It was a cruel woman's voice and it said, *I am coming for you. I will have my crystal.*"

"Oh, Yancy," Destiny said sympathetically and put her hand on his shoulder. They were cousins, and sometimes Destiny could be protective of Yancy, even though he was a teenager and older than us. Maison also stared at him in concern.

But Alex's eyes were elsewhere.

"Look!" she exclaimed, pointing.

I looked, and I couldn't believe it.

CHAPTER 4

THE CRYSTAL SHARD HAD FALLEN ON TOP OF THE gibberish writing in the book. When I looked, I could see right through the crystal—and the words I saw below it were actual words instead of the gibberish from earlier.

"What's going on?" I cried.

Everyone was staring, their mouths hanging open.

"Oh my gosh," Destiny said. "I think I get it." She put her hand on the crystal and began sliding it over the page. Wherever the crystal was, the words below it were readable. As soon as the crystal was off the words, they went back to being gibberish.

"It's like my glasses," Destiny said. "My doctor said that before people made glasses, they cut glass stones and moved them over writing to read it better. It's kind of like that."

"Wow," Yancy said. He still looked shaken from hearing the creepy voice, but this had gotten his attention. "This must have been specially coded so not everyone could read it. What does it say?"

Destiny pushed the crystal shard back to the beginning of the book. "*My name is Steve Alexander,*" she began to read. "*I write this with my own quill pen so the future people of the Overworld can know the truth.*"

"Steve Alexander!" Alex and I cried out in unison.

"Keep reading!" I said.

"*I have been called the greatest hero the Overworld has ever seen,*" Destiny read, slowly moving the crystal shard over the words, "*but I don't feel that way about myself. I have made terrible mistakes, and the Overworld has suffered because I was foolish and full of myself. When I am done writing this book, I will take up my weapon and battle with the Ender Dragon to trap her in the End. But even if I succeed in sealing her there, she could escape one day. If that day ever comes, Overworld will truly be doomed.*"

CHAPTER 5

EVERYONE STARTED TALKING AT ONCE.

Of course! I thought. The Ender Dragon was imprisoned in the End, and these weird happenings must have been her, trying to get out. The crystal shard looked like an Ender crystal, which I knew could also be found in the End. And Endermen had been working for her to try to get the crystal.

Then that voice, that awful voice . . . that must have been the Ender Dragon speaking to me!

I had seen the Ender Dragon once before. When Maison, Alex, Destiny, Yancy, and I were battling the mob Herobrine, we'd transported him to the End for a final battle. The Ender Dragon had been flying ominously overhead. She hadn't spoken to us or attacked us then—so why was she doing it now?

"Okay, okay," Yancy said. "So we know who we're

dealing with now, but there are still lots of questions. Like, why does the Ender Dragon want this crystal shard?"

"Destiny, keep reading," Alex said.

Destiny nervously licked her lips and bent back over the book. "*I will tell about the Ender Dragon's origins at a later date. First I must tell my story, how I plan to imprison the Ender Dragon, and the backup strategy I've come up with in case she ever tries to get out.*"

"Good, good," Yancy said, stroking his chin. "Go on."

"*When I was a child,*" Destiny read, "*the Overworld was a very different place from what it is now. In the present, people are willing to step outside their homes at night. When I was young, no one dared to because it was too dangerous. The Overworld belonged more to the mobs than it did to humans, and the mobs were in a never-ending battle to free the Overworld from humans. They did not want to live in harmony with us.*

"*I was a lonely child,*" Destiny went on. "*The other children learned from their parents how to make houses and wooden swords for protection, but they never tried anything new. Thinking outside the box did not come naturally to them, and I couldn't understand that. I wanted to experiment and see what was just beyond the horizon. I wanted to solve the many mysteries of the Overworld and make it so humans were no longer afraid of the dark. These were noble ideas, but sometimes I would get into* trouble. For instance, when I first tried to tame a wolf, all it did was bite me. The villagers made fun of me and said, 'What did you expect?' But when I did succeed in taming a wolf and turned it into a loyal dog, people started to look at me differently."

"What, is he going to tell us his life story?" Yancy grumbled. "Get to the Ender Dragon!"

"I'm with Yancy," Alex said. "Bor-ing."

"He's probably telling us all this for a reason," Destiny said. "I didn't know that's where dogs came from in the Overworld."

To be honest, neither did I. I realized that even though everyone here knew Steve Alexander's name, there must be a lot of things we didn't know about him.

Destiny bent her head down and read, "*I experimented with putting together rare obsidian rocks and placing fire in the middle of the circle, making a special portal.*"

Yancy's eyes widened. "So he discovered the Nether?"

Destiny nodded and read on. "*The portal led me to a fiery world no one had ever seen before. It had many magical things in it that could be used for more creations, but it also had its own monsters. At first people loved that I discovered the Nether because of the new things they could mine and find in it, but then they grew angry with me when the mobs there attacked them. This was not the only world I discovered by making different portals, but*

I began keeping my discoveries to myself so that I could avoid upsetting people. Most of the portals didn't do anything, though several times I had luck. And the weapons I created with the things I found in other realms helped people better defend themselves. My creation of a diamond sword was especially popular.

"*I found that people were fickle. They loved me and cursed me at the same time. However, no one could deny that I got things done, and some of my discoveries were very popular, like when I figured out how to harness redstone's power. It was because of this that I first became well known in the Overworld, and I was asked to take care of the monster problem. So I rode on my beloved steed into battle.*"

"Steed means horse, right?" I said. Steve Alexander used some fancy words.

"Yeah, I think so," Maison said.

"*Together, we battled against the mobs,*" Destiny read. "*While people had sometimes not liked me before, I soon became famous throughout the land for my many victories. I discovered how water kept Endermen away and how iron doors were the best protection. Over time I started to grow bored, because everything was easily solved with a little brain power.*

"*This was my downfall: thinking I could handle everything and anything myself. When the Ender Dragon decided to destroy the Overworld, I realized nothing I had done prepared me to fight her.*"

"Now we're getting somewhere," Yancy said.

CHAPTER 6

WE FELL SILENT AS DESTINY CONTINUED TO read Steve Alexander's tale.

"*I shudder as I write this,*" Destiny read, "*because I can feel her dark power in my soul. Before her, the mobs of the land each stayed in their own groups. The armed skeletons all worked together, the zombies helped other zombies, and the Endermen kept to themselves. But the Ender Dragon wanted to become the queen of all mobs. She planned to lead her wicked army of mobs against all the humans of the Overworld and wipe us out once and for all.*

"*As her power grew, she was able to change our very world. Night grew longer, giving her mobs more time to attack villagers and wreak havoc. She blasted through whole villages for her own entertainment, letting her minions run after the fleeing villagers. Everyone was in a terror.*

"*I knew the only way to stop this was to stop the leader, to take out the Ender Dragon herself. No weapons or person in the Overworld was strong enough to defeat her, so I searched realms like the Nether, trying to find something. It was in my desperation that I discovered the End, a desolate place where Endermen spawned. I thought it would be the perfect prison. But I needed new tools and enchantments to trap the Ender Dragon there.*

"*One day, while I was down in the Nether, I discovered blocks I'd never seen before, and I wondered if they had any special properties. After several attempts, something changed. The middle of a portal I made began to glow green, blue, and red. It seemed to beckon me. I had no idea what lay beyond it, but still I plunged into the portal and came out into a strange world. A world called Earth.*"

CHAPTER 7

DESTINY HAD TO STOP READING BECAUSE EVERY-
one was talking again.

"He did find Earth!" Alex was practically hyperventilating. "That must be why we found the image of that Earth woman in the wall!"

"There's still more," Destiny told us, and we all fell silent again to listen.

She read, "*You can imagine my shock when I first saw this ugly land.*"

"Hey," Yancy and Maison said, insulted.

But Destiny kept going. "*In all of the other realms I'd visited, creatures maintained their normal, blocky shape. Here, however, people were shaped differently, and so were animals. The land came in all different shapes as opposed to being normal blocks. For a while I stood there* staring in stunned disgust at this new land. And that's when the woman attacked me.

"She had a long stick that she used as a weapon, and she struck out at me, yelling to get away from her home. I dodged the long stick and fell back. I held up my hands, shouting that I wasn't from here and I didn't mean her any harm. The woman huffed and put her stick down, waiting impatiently for me to explain myself. That was the first time I realized this was another human, because I recognized the expressions on her face, even if her body was shaped all wrong. Apparently I looked as strange to her as she did to me, and she thought I was some sort of monster because of how I appeared.

"I explained that I did come from another world, but I was not a monster. This made the woman look even more suspicious. She pointed her stick at me and asked why I had come.

"I said I was in desperate need because a dragon was destroying my world. She sighed and said her world did not have to deal with dragons, but they had other issues. It turned out she was one of the leaders in her community, and they had been suffering from a famine and had nothing to eat. I told her that food was no issue, and I could bring her food from my land. She said that if I did, she would help me in my quest to defeat the dragon.

"She called herself Maya, and I introduced myself as Steve Alexander. As it turned out, that surprise meeting *would be helpful to both of our people, and the woman and I would become close friends.*

"After her people had feasted on the first food I presented and had what they needed to eat and drink, Maya asked to learn more about the dragon. Together we experimented with the tools available to us from the Overworld, the Nether, and Earth.

"After many attempts, Maya and I came up with something together. We created a specially enchanted Ender crystal. There are two kinds of Ender crystal I know of: the kind in the End, which I believe the Ender Dragon can use to keep her health up. I've accepted the fact that she can use the Ender crystal for her own purposes in the End—so long as she remains imprisoned. But this Ender crystal was different, because of the enchantments used. It is the most powerful weapon I have ever created—far more powerful than a thousand diamond swords or a world full of redstone.

"Maya has offered to help me take up arms in the upcoming battle with the Ender Dragon. But I would feel too guilty letting her risk her life for my world. I told her I had other ideas. In case the Ender Dragon ever tries to escape in the future, I have asked Maya to break up the crystal as soon as the battle is over. She is to hide the shards in different places. We are enchanting this book together, so it can help lead a worthy person to those shards, but they will have great difficulty finding all the pieces. The more shards that are found, the more pages of this book

will be revealed. I have asked Maya to bury the first shard of the crystal near my home, in hopes my descendants will find them if they are needed.

"*It is our hope that this crystal will never be needed again. But if the Ender Dragon ever grows strong enough to escape the End, these crystal pieces must all be found and put together to recreate my ultimate weapon.*

"*I feel it is too dangerous for most of the people of the Overworld to know about Maya, Earth, and the Ender crystal weapon. If and when I trap the Ender Dragon in the End, I have asked Maya to do more than take care of this book and the crystal. For her safety and for her world, I have asked her to destroy the portal I made to Earth. Earth isn't as ugly as I originally believed, and I have to admit my heart cracks at the thought that I might never see my best friend again. But it must be done.*

"*Anyone who reads this, beware. You have stumbled upon greater magic and evil than you have ever known. I cannot stress enough how much the enchanted Ender crystal is a double-edged sword. I hope to use it to save our world, but it can do much more. Not only can it be used by bad humans for bad gains, but it can also be used by the Ender Dragon herself. She will want all the crystals too, not only to keep the one weapon that can possibly defeat her in her clutches, but also to help her in her quest to destroy the Overworld.*

"*Soon I must prepare to fight. I know the Ender Dragon is expecting a world-shattering battle, and she has already vowed revenge on me and on my descendants. And so I will say goodbye to Maya, to my wife, and to my young son, Steve. If I don't make it out of this, I love you all."*

CHAPTER 8

MY HEARTBEAT WAS POUNDING IN MY EARS, and I didn't think I was the only one feeling that way. "What does it say next?" I blurted.

"It shows a map," Destiny said, moving the crystal shard over the pages. "After that, it's all gibberish again."

"Let me see." Alex shoved her way in, taking the crystal shard from Destiny. Sure enough, all the words that came after this were gibberish, even with the crystal placed directly over them.

"Maybe we have to find the next crystal before we can read more," Maison said. "Is that what it meant when it said 'The more shards that are found, the more pages of this book will be revealed'?"

"But how do we find the next shard?" Yancy asked.

"It must be the map," I said. Alex was so busy

running the crystal over the gibberish that I thought she'd forgotten about the map. Then again, who could blame her? All of our heads were probably whirring from all the information we'd taken in. I knew my brain was jumping from thought to thought. Steve Alexander really was my ancestor! There'd been a portal to Earth way back in the past! And . . . and . . .

And the Ender Dragon was our new enemy. She'd vowed revenge on Steve Alexander and his descendants, which meant she would go after Alex and me especially.

I quickly took the crystal back and put it over the space that had revealed a map. Landmarks appeared, tinted faintly purple from the crystal.

"I know where this is!" I exclaimed.

Alex looked closely at the map, and she recognized it too.

"It's a map to Herobrine's temple," she said. "We have to get that next crystal shard!"

CHAPTER 9

THE FIVE OF US HAD BEEN TO HEROBRINE'S TEMple before. It wasn't really *Herobrine's* temple, but we called it that because we'd faced off against Herobrine there. It was a temple on a mountain surrounded by a dark forest, and it had been there for so long that no one knew who'd originally created it or why. These days the temple was partly in ruins because it had been abandoned for so long.

Alex wanted to leave right away, but I said, "We have to wait for my dad to get back."

"Stevie, really?" Alex said. "*We're* the Overworld Heroes. We need to take care of this right away!"

Alex's mom, my Aunt Alexandra, was the mayor of a nearby village, and she had recently dubbed Alex, Maison, Destiny, Yancy, and me the Overworld Heroes task force. Aunt Alexandra was supposed to call on us whenever something bad or fishy happened in the Overworld. "Bad" and "fishy" definitely described this whole situation, but Aunt Alexandra hadn't given us any orders yet. Of course, she couldn't give us orders if we couldn't tell her what was going on—but Dad had told me not to leave the house, and he was a stickler for rules. It was hard to be part of a task force as an eleven-year-old.

"I agree with Alex," Yancy said. "Those Endermen before were really aggressive trying to find the first crystal shard. They're definitely hunting for the other shards. Maybe we can get them all before the Ender Dragon's mobs do."

"Or maybe the Ender Dragon's mobs are already there," I said, "and it'd be better to wait until my dad gets back."

"We could compromise," Maison said. "Let's leave your dad a note, saying this is an emergency and telling him where we're going. He can follow after he gets home and reads it. Besides, it takes more than half a day to walk to that temple from here. If we leave now, we can make it before nightfall. If we wait for your dad, we might have to wait until tomorrow."

Alex waved the book in front of my face. "This is way more dangerous than we ever thought," she said. "Did you hear what Destiny read? The Ender Dragon wants those same crystal shards, and what if she gets them before us?"

"Bye-bye, Overworld," Yancy said bluntly.

I still didn't think Dad would be very pleased. But he would probably prefer that we save the Overworld rather than let it get destroyed. And Maison was right that our mission would be a lot safer in the day, though there was still the threat of Endermen, who could be out in the light.

I also thought of Steve Alexander and tried to think of what he would do. He'd said he was foolish and full of himself, but I couldn't believe that. He wouldn't be our greatest hero if that was true, and he wouldn't have trapped the Ender Dragon. If the rest of the Overworld looked up to him, he had to be a good person for me to follow in the footsteps of. And if danger reared its head, I doubted Steve Alexander waited and asked his dad what to do.

"Okay," I said. "Let's pack some supplies and I'll write my dad a note. We'll leave the first crystal shard here." Since Endermen could sense the crystal shard if they got close enough, we might accidentally attract mobs if we carried the crystal with us. And since we knew the way to the temple, we could leave the book behind, too.

While the others rushed to gather food for our health and weapons for self-defense, I wrote Dad a note. Then I had a really, truly terrible thought: When the Ender Dragon promised to go after Steve Alexander's descendants, my first thought had been Alex and me.

We were the youngest generation. But we weren't the only living descendants. If Alex and I were in danger, so were Dad and Aunt Alexandra. Was it dangerous for Dad to be out all by himself right now?

Normally I'd never worry about Dad on his own because he's such a skilled mob slayer. But if he was caught off-guard and overwhelmed . . . if the Ender Dragon went after him first . . .

At the end of the note, I wrote, *Please be safe.* Something I never thought I'd have to say to Dad. Then I grabbed my diamond sword and ran out the door with the others.

Together, we sprinted in the direction of Herobrine's temple.

CHAPTER 10

I T WAS A LONG TREK TO THE TEMPLE. I KEPT MY EYES on the sky, keeping track of the time of day based on the position of the sun. Jagged, boxy clouds moved lazily over the blue sky as the sun shone down, the world alive with green grass and flowers. It was such a beautiful world. Why would the Ender Dragon want to destroy it?

Of course, the Overworld wasn't all she wanted to destroy. She wanted to destroy my family—and me, specifically. Because of what someone else had done. That was how deep her hatred was.

What kind of a being was she? Steve Alexander had talked about his childhood, but he hadn't said where the Ender Dragon came from. He said he'd get to that later. I wondered why, because it seemed like that could be pretty useful information. If I knew the

Ender Dragon's origin, it might also give me details on her weaknesses and how she thought. It was clear she was not a mindless monster like most of the mobs I'd dealt with.

The sun began to sneak down toward the horizon. That meant the day was more than halfway over. The shadows started to slant and grow longer, like evil hands reaching out.

When we got to the forests surrounding the mountain, we could see the temple. From where we were the temple looked small and unimportant. The trees were close together.

We spotted them before they saw us—armed skeletons, walking in the shade, looking around.

"I'll get it!" Alex said, pulling out her bow and arrows. She tied a lead onto one of the arrows and shot the arrow on top of the nearest tree. Then we all climbed up the lead and onto the treetops.

"Hey, I've been wondering," Yancy said as we began walking from tree to tree. "What happened to Steve Alexander after he put the Ender Dragon in the End?"

"He had a world-shattering battle with the Ender Dragon. We've been talking for centuries about how he saved all of us from her!" Alex said triumphantly.

"Yeah, but what happened to him afterward?" Yancy said. "Did he get hurt? Did he find a way home? What?"

Alex frowned, not so excited. "Hmm, I don't know."

"There are a lot of Steve Alexander stories," I said, "but I don't know either. It's kind of like all the stories stop after he defeated the Ender Dragon."

I paused. He hadn't really defeated her. But he had saved us from her for a long period of time. In the book, Steve Alexander didn't sound too sure of himself sometimes, which I found funny. How could the greatest hero of the Overworld have doubted himself? Did he not think much of himself because he hadn't been able to defeat the Ender Dragon entirely?

"He said he'd never see Maya again," Yancy went on. "What about his wife and son? Did he make it out of the battle? Did he have to go into the End to make sure the dragon got there? In the *Minecraft* game, you can't get out of the End until you win in a battle against the Ender Dragon. So then—"

Alex and I still didn't have any real answers, but that didn't stop her from speaking up. "Of course he made it out of the battle," Alex said. "We don't know exactly what happened, but if he didn't make it out of the battle, we would definitely have heard about it."

"I never heard of anything bad happening to his wife or kid, either," I said. "So I guess it must have all worked out. Except that now . . ."

We all walked quietly for a moment, lost in our thoughts.

Finally, Alex broke the silence. "The map didn't say *where* in the temple you can find the crystal shard. So we might have to do a lot of searching."

I hadn't thought about that. We all looked at one another and sped up, wanting to get to the temple as fast as possible. I kept watching the sun in the sky.

When we got to the top of the mountain, the temple looked exactly the same as it had the last time I'd been there. "Spread out," Alex said. "We have a better chance of finding the crystal that way."

We started by searching the ground and under blocks and columns. Nothing. It wouldn't have been safe to leave it in so obvious a place, so where had Steve Alexander stuck it? Was it in a mineshaft under the mountain, like where I'd found the first crystal shard?

I looked down the mountain. It was a long way down, which meant there was a lot of area where there might have been a mineshaft. This reminded me of an Earth saying Maison had taught me: "Like finding a needle in a haystack." We could stay here for days and still not find anything.

I pulled out my pickaxe and hit it repeatedly into the rocky mountainside. The pickaxe made a comforting *thwack-thwack* sound as it broke up blocks of mountain. The others also got busy with their weapons, clearing away space.

"This is hopeless," Destiny said, wiping sweat off her forehead with the back of her hand.

"Are you sure the book didn't say anything else about where it was hidden?" Alex asked.

"You read it, too," Destiny reminded her.

"Hey, I think I found something!" Maison called out excitedly.

We ran over to see. Maison was kneeling before a block of mountain, and she pointed at it. The letters S and A could be seen etched into the block, but just barely. The carving was so small we all squinted and wondered if we were imagining it.

"The S and A seems to be his mark," Maison said, digging down farther. Her pickaxe made quick work of the block. She struck the block below the carved one, while we all went after the blocks nearby. Hopefully that crystal was around here somewhere!

I took a moment to look up at the sky. What were we going to do once it became dark? If we found the crystal now, we might be able to make it to the edge of the forest before sunset. Maybe. It'd be cutting it close, and we definitely wouldn't be anywhere near home. Where was Dad? I kept wishing he'd catch up with us. He could help us, and . . .

. . . And if he arrived, I'd know the Ender Dragon hadn't gotten to him. Flushed, I worked harder with my pickaxe. The *thwack-thwack* sound got less comforting and started to sound more desperate.

After a while, Maison's face fell. "Maybe I was

wrong," she said. "I could have sworn I saw those let-ters in the block."

"It's okay, Maison," Yancy said. "We'll just all spread out again."

Maison continued to dig by the S-A block while the rest of us stepped away. Her face was flushed, as if she needed to prove that the crystal was where she'd thought it would be.

I returned to where I'd been digging before. My head was lowered, but I felt it when a long shadow fell over me, darkening my space. I looked up in shock. Someone—something—else had joined us on the mountaintop.

"An Enderman!" I cried.

CHAPTER 11

AS SOON AS I SAID IT, THE ENDERMAN VANISHED. Teleportation was one of the special skills Endermen had, making it very easy for them to sneak up on people, and very hard for people to pin them to one area and defeat them.

I spun around, looking for the mob, my diamond sword at the ready. Everyone else had jumped at the sound of my voice and they were searching for it too.

There it was! It had reappeared next to Maison, looming over her. Maison swung at it with her pickaxe and the Enderman disappeared and reappeared several feet away.

Alex pulled back her bow and sent an arrow flying. But by the time the arrow hit its mark, the Enderman was long gone. It showed up again right behind Maison, knocking her out of the way. We all went running toward it, and the Enderman reached down and moved blocks, hurriedly pushing them out of the way. Maison got back up on her feet and swung for the Enderman just as the rest of us were reaching the area.

For a split second I thought I saw something shining in the Enderman's long hands. Then the Enderman was gone, vanishing just in time to miss Maison's pickaxe. It appeared a moment later on another part of the mountaintop, and I could definitely see something purple in its hands.

The new crystal shard!

"Don't let it get away!" I shouted, running at it with my sword held high. Maison had been right about the S and A in the block, and this Enderman had swooped in when she'd almost had it!

Everyone was going for the Enderman at once, but that only helped the mob. Because when we all reached it, the Enderman vanished and appeared on another part of the mountaintop far away. This wasn't going to work!

The Enderman turned away from us, and that gave Alex an opportunity. Her arrow flew through the air and struck the Enderman's back, making its body turn red and freeze for an instant. Then another arrow went flying and we had enough time to all run and jump on the Enderman. The crystal shard fell on the ground, so I knew we'd defeated the Enderman for good. The crystal was so beautiful, and so small. You'd never guess what power it held just by looking at it.

I was the first to reach the crystal shard and I snatched it up. "Got it!" I said triumphantly, holding it up so everyone could see.

"I knew it said S and A!" Maison said, her face lit up.

Yancy looked warily at the spot where the Enderman had last stood. "We better hurry up and get out of here," he said. "If there was one, there might be others coming. And now that we've got the crystal, we're sitting ducks."

I quickly ducked, thinking that was a direction.

Yancy shook his head at me and said, "We have to get you out more often."

Maison stopped smiling, realizing he was right. "At least we have the crystal," she said.

"And there's an old, abandoned house not far from here," Alex said. "We can hide there for the night."

We hurried across the mountaintop, eager to get back up in the trees for safety. I looked back behind me and saw the sun slipping closer to the horizon. It would be dark before we even reached the abandoned house. And even if we found shelter, if enough Endermen knew where we were, they could tear the house to pieces to get to us. And the crystal.

CHAPTER 12

WE WERE ALMOST AT THE EDGE OF THE TREES when the sun dipped below the horizon, turning everything dark. I could hear the sounds of mobs nearby. Zombies moaning. The hissing of skeletons.

Alex pulled a torch out of her toolkit to help us see, and Destiny carried it so that Alex could hold onto her bow and arrows. With monsters nearby, we all wanted Alex to have her arrows ready.

"Here," Alex said. She'd found the lead she'd tied to the tree earlier, and we used it to get back down to the ground. Maison, Destiny, and Yancy had a lot of trouble with the rope, because this wasn't something they normally did in their world. It was even harder for them in the dark.

Come on, come on, I thought as I watched them climb down. *We have to move!*

The darkness made the crystal's glow really obvious in my hand—the whole area around us was washed in violet light. Even from far away, someone would be able to see it.

Finally, everyone made it back down to the ground. Looking back into the forest, I could see mobs milling around. Skeletons snuck behind trees, their arrows ready. Zombies lurched. Giant spiders crawled around the tree trunks, their red eyes shining eerily in the crystal's light. I wondered what Steve Alexander's world had originally been like, if the world we lived in now was a big improvement compared to what he'd been used to.

With one last look at the mobs, we tore off again.

Because it was night now, I knew there was probably no way we'd reach the house before some sort of mob attacked us. Thankfully the ones in the forest were far enough away to leave us alone, but there was a chance that we'd run into hostile mobs at any moment. The night was alive with their hisses and moans.

The next thing I knew, there was an Enderman in front of me, blocking my path.

I bellowed and screeched to a stop. The Enderman quickly advanced on me, its long black arms reaching out for the crystal. Little sizzles of purple light were hovering around the Enderman, almost matching the light of the crystal.

The others all rushed to charge the Enderman and it disappeared. I spun around, looking for it.

"Just run, Stevie!" Maison shouted.

She was right! Looking for the Enderman would only take up more time, and there was no doubt the mob would show up again. We all started running, but then two Endermen appeared in our path, stopping us again.

Alex shot arrows to take care of them. The Endermen vanished just in the nick of time and reappeared a second later. Two more appeared out of the darkness behind them, coming our way.

Yes, yes, get the crystal! a familiar voice roared in my head. *Bring it back to me!*

The evil in the Ender Dragon's voice was so strong it felt like a physical blow. My knees almost buckled under me. I caught myself from falling and stared in front of me in shock, because dozens of Endermen had suddenly appeared, circling around us as though to cage us in.

Without even thinking about it, Maison, Alex, Destiny, Yancy, and I all pulled closer together in the middle of the circle, holding our weapons.

"What do we do?" Destiny whispered frantically.

Alex eyed the Endermen angrily. "I can start shooting them with my arrows if you can finish them off."

She sent arrows flying, but the Endermen were expecting it. Every time she released an arrow, they'd disappear just long enough for the arrow to miss them, then they'd reappear a second later in the exact same spot. All Alex was doing was wasting her arrows. We were trapped.

Then it was like someone had given the Endermen a signal, because they all disappeared at once and reappeared in a cluster just inches from us. There were rows and rows of Endermen penning us in. I was desperately slashing out at them with my diamond sword, but it didn't do any good.

Finally one Enderman lurched even closer to me and snatched the crystal right out of my hands. And then they all disappeared. I looked everywhere around us for it to show back up, because the crystal's glow would be a perfect giveaway. But the glow was nowhere to be seen. Wherever the Enderman had gone, it had taken the crystal with it. And wherever it had gone, that crystal would soon be in the clutches of the Ender Dragon.

We had failed.

CHAPTER 13

THE OTHER ENDERMEN STARTED TO BACK AWAY, like they knew their mission was complete. A few completely disappeared. Some stayed, but they no longer paid any attention to us—they just milled around with their long arms swinging.

"No!" I wailed. I looked at the others and I knew the devastation on their faces must have been reflected on mine. I could tell they didn't know what to do, either.

"Is there some way to track the crystal?" Destiny cried.

"The book was supposed to help us track it," Alex said. "But it could be anywhere now."

"Anywhere?" Yancy said. "No way. If it's not in the End yet, it's going to be."

Think, Stevie, think! I ordered myself. Fighting

battles wasn't just about might, it was also about strategy. That's how we'd been victorious in the past. But what kind of strategy could help us find a missing Enderman?

Then I thought of something.

"If I could *be* an Enderman, maybe I could track the Enderman that has the crystal!" I exclaimed.

Everyone looked at me. Even though it was dark out I could see they thought I wasn't making any sense.

"Remember?" I said. "When the Endermen were searching for the first crystal shard, they were turning villagers into Endermen to help them look. Maybe if I turn into an Enderman, I'll be able to sense where the crystal is and get it back."

"But the people who turned into Endermen were brainwashed to think like Endermen," Yancy said. "If you turn into one, you wouldn't be Stevie anymore. You might even want to *help* the Ender Dragon."

My excitement deflated. Yancy was right!

"Still, it might be the best chance we have," Maison said. "We have the first crystal. And then maybe we can use it to turn Stevie back into a human."

"If we can get Stevie to go back home and make sure to touch him with the crystal, like with the villager Endermen before," Yancy said. The dryness of his voice told me he didn't think any of this would work. "Like Stevie as an Enderman would really just let us lead him home peacefully? He'll just disappear on us."

"He might want to go back to his house because he'll sense that first crystal, too," Maison argued. "And the villagers who got turned into Endermen didn't start to think entirely like Endermen—at least not right away. They said there was still some part of themselves in there."

"They also said that part kept fading, and they would have turned fully into Endermen if we hadn't saved them in time," Yancy said.

I looked back and forth between my friends as they argued. They both had good points. My heart was pounding so hard I was surprised the others couldn't hear it. *Think, Stevie!* I ordered myself, but I couldn't think of anything else. There wasn't time to wait for Dad to follow our note and find us. We didn't even know where he was, or if he was okay. And I couldn't come up with any other way to track the Enderman with the crystal.

"I have to do this," I said. "You guys just stick close to me and make sure I turn back before I lose myself."

Before they could talk me out of it, I ran into the arms of the nearest Enderman and let myself be caught.

CHAPTER 14

I T WAS LIKE BEING SWALLOWED UP BY THE NIGHT. Everything went so pitch black I couldn't have seen my own hands in front of me. And it was so, so cold.

My mind blurred. Where was I? What was I doing? I'd been on a mission, and it was really important. I just couldn't remember what it was.

I saw something purple in my mind.

Oh.

The crystal shard. I had to get the crystal shard.

Yes, Stevie, said the voice in my head. Why had I thought that voice was evil? I mean, it was kind of spooky, but I also wanted to obey it. The voice belonged to someone really powerful and queenly. Obeying it felt right.

Be a good boy, Stevie, the voice went on. This was the most it had ever talked to me, so I must have been special to it now. I could tell it liked me. *I know who you are. Come, you shouldn't fight me. It's better to be on my side.*

Yes, your highness, I thought back.

The blackness started to fade around me. It was still dark, but I realized that, even though it was nighttime, I could see some things. There were other Endermen nearby. Hey, Endermen like me! There was a redheaded Overworld girl with arrows, and a few funny-looking kids who didn't look like they were from around here. I could see the outlines of dark trees and sense everything that was around me. Wait, why hadn't I sensed things this well before? Hadn't I always been an Enderman?

I could see a lot of blocks nearby. They would be fun to grab and move around. I looked down at my body. For some reason I didn't remember being this tall. My arms were really long, perfect for reaching for things. I was holding a diamond sword, which was pretty weird, because I didn't think Endermen like me used swords.

"Stevie?" one of the funny-looking kids said. She got up close and looked me right in the eye. "This is Maison. Are you in there, Stevie?"

Maison. That sounded sort of familiar. I couldn't remember why, though. I needed to find more crystal shards and bring them to my queen. I pushed past Maison and looked around. Part of me wanted to attack her since she'd looked in my eyes, but finding the crystal shards was even more important to me. Too bad. It would be fun to attack a human.

The redheaded girl jumped in front of me and raised her bow. Silly girl. I could just teleport away. Wait, that sounded like a good idea.

I teleported and reappeared a short distance away. It was like blinking and opening my eyes to find I was somewhere else. Somehow my mind had decided where I wanted to teleport to, and then it had happened.

The kids ran back in front of me. Why wouldn't they leave me alone? They were so annoying.

"This is what I was afraid of!" The tallest kid was talking now. "He doesn't remember anything, and we'll never be able to get him back. Stevie! Hey, Stevie!" He hollered the last bit in my face.

Boy, he was so annoying! I teleported again to be away from him.

I appeared a few feet away and the annoying kids still followed me. It was like they knew me or something!

The girl who had spoken to me first got in front of me again. "Stevie!" she shouted. "You have to be in there somewhere! Don't you remember me? I'm your best friend. We have a portal so we can go to the Overworld and Earth. Don't you remember?"

I wanted to tell her to leave me alone. I needed to find crystal shards! But when I started to talk, I realized I couldn't. I just made a hissing sound. That was pretty weird, because I remembered being able to talk before. No, wait. That didn't make any sense, because I'd always been an Enderman. Right? I needed to find those crystals!

"Stevie!" the redheaded girl yelled. She wasn't trying to sound nice like the other girl. This girl just sounded irritated. "It's Alex, your cousin! We went to the Nether together, remember? We defeated Herobrine!"

How could I have a cousin who was a human? Shouldn't my cousins be Endermen?

The other two kids jumped in front of me, too. "Stevie, you used to hate me, remember?" the tall boy said. "Because when we first met, I liked to bully people online. But then we became friends. Remember when I made you peanut butter and jelly sandwiches? Remember all the times I've put a Jack o' Lantern on my head?"

He would look pretty funny with a Jack o' Lantern on his head. I wondered why he would do that.

"Please, Stevie!" the last girl said. She was holding a torch and wearing funny pieces of glass on her face. Wait, hadn't she been talking about reading words with glasses earlier? No, that couldn't be right. How could that be something I'd remember?

I was getting ready to teleport again when the girl who called herself Maison stood in front of me. She had her legs set wide apart, like she was making sure I couldn't move her aside. Her eyes were much smaller than the eyes of people in the Overworld, but they were so full of some kind of emotion that it made them look big and watery.

"Not so fast, Stevie," she said. "There must be something you remember."

And she held up her hands to me.

CHAPTER 15

INGERS! THOSE CRAZY THINGS THEY HAD ON Earth but we didn't have in the Overworld! Hold on a second—how did I know that?

She began wiggling her fingers, and I stared at them. Didn't I once think they looked like squid tentacles? Well, I still kind of did, but I wasn't going to tell her that. Why wasn't I going to tell her? Oh, because I liked her. Wait, why was that?

Stevie! The voice was in my head again. *Ignore them! Bring me my crystals!*

The voice made me shudder. It was so evil! Why had I thought it was okay to listen to it just a few moments ago? I lifted my long arms and put them over my face, trying to clear my head. I had so many thoughts and images jumping around in my mind that I couldn't keep any of them straight.

"He seems to be responding!" the boy said. He and the other funny-looking girl with the pieces of glass on her face began wiggling their fingers, too. I stared hard.

Maison, I thought. *Yancy. Destiny.* I looked at the redheaded girl, who wasn't wiggling her fingers because she didn't have any. *Alex.*

I remembered them!

Right at that moment, I realized I could sense where the missing ender crystal shard was. It was on the other side of the mountain. The Enderman who'd gotten it was holding it there. Soon it would head back to the End and present the crystal to the Ender Dragon.

I had to get the crystal back—before it was too late!

I looked at the other kids. I couldn't just leave them here with so many mobs around. I didn't think any mobs would attack me in my new form, so I gestured for them to climb on my back.

"Uh, what's going on?" Yancy asked.

"I think he understands!" Maison said. "He wants us to jump on his back."

"Why?" Yancy said. "So he can eat us?"

"No, look," Maison said. "When he first changed, his eyes were purple like an Enderman's. Now they look like . . . like Stevie's eyes."

"He's as tall as an Enderman," Alex said. "Before, when the other villagers changed into Endermen, they weren't that tall."

"Maybe it affects people in different ways," Maison said.

While they were talking about this, we were losing time to get the crystal back. I gestured more forcefully for them to climb on my back.

Yancy let out a long sigh. "Here goes nothing."

They all grabbed on to me. If I were in my Stevie body, I never would have been able to handle all that weight. But in my Enderman body it didn't bother me at all.

I teleported up the mountain. When I reappeared, I checked to make sure everyone was still hanging on to me. They were, but they looked a little out of breath. Teleporting for them was harder than teleporting for me. I remembered how hard it was when an Enderman had grabbed me before and teleported with me. It had been stressful, and I hadn't been able to breathe during teleportation. But it was still better than teleporting with an Ender pearl, because those had really lowered my health.

Hang on, I thought. I teleported again.

Together, we made it to the other side of the mountain. Standing a few feet away from us was the Enderman with the crystal shard. The Enderman looked transfixed, as if the shard had some kind of power over it.

"There it is!" Destiny said.

All of them leapt off my back. I hurried toward the Enderman, knowing this was my last chance.

CHAPTER 16

THE ENDERMAN TURNED TOWARD US, HISSING. IT knew it would battle us to protect the crystal. But its eyes were on me, so it didn't notice when Alex pulled back her bowstring. Her arrow flew through the air and hit the Enderman.

The Enderman flashed red and I teleported right next to it. I snatched the crystal back! The Enderman hissed and tried to take it, but another of Alex's arrows hit it right on its square head. While it was trying to recover, Maison, Destiny, and Yancy lunged for the Enderman, taking it out with their weapons.

"I can't believe that actually worked," Yancy said.

"We did it, Stevie!" Maison cheered. "We have the crystal back."

I stopped listening. What a beautiful crystal! I held

it in my long arms, studying it. This was a crystal fit for a queen. In fact . . .

Yes, Stevie, said the voice in my head. It didn't sound angry anymore. I decided I didn't mind it. *Bring me the crystal, Stevie. It's not too late.*

I needed to teleport to the End and give the crystal to her! That had been my mission all along. I looked at the strange humans around me. I couldn't remember why they were here.

One of the girl humans gasped. "Oh no!" she said. "Stevie's eyes have gone purple again! Stevie, Stevie, it's me, Maison! Look!" She started wiggling things on her hands. They looked like little squid tentacles. Why would I want to see that? I needed to get this crystal shard to my queen!

"Stevie, no!" The boy tried to tackle me by jumping on my back. I easily brushed him off.

Look at them, Stevie, the voice said. *They want to keep you from bringing the crystal to me, even though it's rightfully mine! Do you know what I need you to do?*

What, my queen? I asked in my head.

Her answer came to me immediately:

Destroy them.

CHAPTER 17

I TURNED ON THE PESKY KIDS.

Yes, my queen! I thought.

The redheaded girl pulled her arrow back. "Don't make me do this, Stevie!" she shouted.

Stevie? Who was Stevie? That name sounded almost like Steve Alexander. Why did I know that name?

When I thought about Steve Alexander's name, I felt the Ender Dragon shudder, like something had hurt her.

Don't think of him! she ordered.

I tried to figure out why that name had made my queen so angry. How could a name have that much power? The kids all crowded closer, calling me "Stevie" again and again.

"No descendant of Steve Alexander is going to be a servant of the Ender Dragon!" the redheaded girl said hotly. "Steve Alexander is the greatest hero the Overworld has ever seen. Don't you dare let him down like this."

Wait . . . In my mind I could see a statue of a man holding a diamond sword. That was Steve Alexander. And I was his . . . descendant?

Don't listen to them! the Ender Dragon warned. Even though her voice was in my head, it sounded so loud that I couldn't help thinking everyone must be able to hear her. *They lie to you! I'm the one telling you the truth! Bring me my crystal!*

I tried to think of what truth she was telling me. All I knew was that she wanted this crystal and I wanted to obey her.

But something didn't feel right.

"You're not an Enderman!" the black-haired girl said. Her voice was forceful, full of real feelings and desperation. "You're Stevie! You're getting the crystal away from the Ender Dragon and her Endermen. Because she'll destroy all of us if she gets the crystal back."

The crystal pulsed in my arms, as if it had a heartbeat. Then, suddenly, from deep within the crystal, I heard another voice—just barely. It was a man's voice, and very deep. *Return to your friends, Stevie,* it said. *I am watching over you in your mission. Don't fall into her trap!*

Silence! the Ender Dragon roared.

Something in my head shattered like glass. I blinked, and suddenly I remembered who and what I was. I was Stevie, the son of Steve and descendant of Steve Alexander! I wasn't the servant of the Ender Dragon. She could never have this crystal!

"His eyes are back to normal!" Maison exclaimed.

The man's voice seemed to have left the crystal, but the Ender Dragon's hadn't. *Get him!* she hollered. I realized she was calling out to all the Endermen and mobs in the area, sending them after me. *Get him, and get that crystal!*

I looked around. Endermen were quickly teleporting toward me. Armed skeletons came out from under the trees. The air filled with moans as zombies came our way. We were surrounded.

I gestured for everyone to get on my back again, and this time they didn't hesitate. Then I teleported, disappearing just before the mobs reached us.

CHAPTER 18

"**T**HE HOUSE IS THAT WAY!" ALEX LEANED OVER MY shoulder and pointed to the left.

That's when I remembered we were all supposed to go hide in an abandoned house tonight. It was like my mind was clearing after hearing the man's voice. I didn't know for sure whose voice I had heard, but I could guess.

Again and again I teleported in the direction of the abandoned house, making sure to keep disappearing just as soon as we'd appeared in a spot. I hoped this made it harder for the Ender Dragon's mobs to follow us.

But all the teleporting was really hard on my friends. I heard them gasping for breath and clinging to me with shaking limbs. I knew they couldn't hold on for much longer.

What should I do? I could make it to the house, but I was scared the Endermen would just follow me there. So I started teleporting a little out of the way, trying to confuse them.

"No, Stevie!" Alex shouted. Then we teleported and she couldn't say anything else. When we reappeared, she said, "That way!"

Too bad I couldn't talk to tell her my plan. I really was trying to help!

After a few fake teleports that I knew made my friends really uneasy, I got back on track. I headed in the direction of the house. Finally, we could see the house in front of us. It was so small, barely a shack. But it would have to work.

"Oh, thank goodness!" Maison slid off my back and I could see she was trembling. All four of them were. "I thought all that teleporting was going to make me sick."

Alex hurried over to the front door and opened it. We burst inside and slammed the door behind us.

"First things first," Maison said. She reached out for the crystal shard, which I still had in my long hands.

No, mine! I thought. I wanted to keep the crystal for myself.

Then Maison pulled it from my hands. She reached up and touched my shoulder with the crystal.

There was a blinding explosion of purple light, and suddenly I felt different. Turning back to a human was way better than turning into an Enderman. It wasn't so cold and scary and dark. I felt myself getting shorter and warmer and the mixed-up thoughts all cleared from my head. It was like waking up and realizing those scary thoughts had just been nightmares.

Except it had been real. I'd really felt all of that. I'd really wanted to obey the Ender Dragon.

The purple light went away and left me standing there, unharmed. I checked my brown arms and my turquoise shirt and blue pants. Everything looked normal.

Maison sagged with relief. "That was really scary for a while. What happened?"

Alex, meanwhile, peered out the window at the night. "So far I don't see anything following us. Let's sit down so they can't see us through the window."

Destiny was setting the torch on the wall so we could all see. At the same time, Yancy reached into his toolkit and pulled out food and milk.

"I think we all need this for our health, too," Yancy said. "Stevie looks pretty wiped out. He can tell us what it felt like after we have a bite to eat."

I didn't argue. I was still sifting through the thoughts I'd had while I was an Enderman. I wasn't proud of how I'd acted some of the time.

We all sat down, exhausted, and ate the food. I watched as my friends' pale faces filled up with color while they ate. That was good, because it meant their health was getting better. Pretty soon they had all their health back.

"I understand why people obey the Ender Dragon," I said finally, thinking of the villager Endermen I'd met. It was hard to admit.

Everyone looked at me as if I were crazy.

"The Ender Dragon wants to destroy this world!" Yancy said. "Why would anyone want to obey her?"

It had all been really obvious to me in the moment. Now I realized I was going to have a hard time explaining it. "Her power is just so strong," I said. "I think the things keeping me from obeying her while I was an Enderman were you guys . . . and . . . a voice."

Everyone looked concerned now.

"A good voice!" I quickly explained. "I heard the Ender Dragon's voice, and she was talking to me more than ever, telling me to give her the crystal. But there was also a man's voice. I think it was . . ." I hesitated. I didn't know if I was right. "I think it was Steve Alexander."

"Steve Alexander spoke to you!?" Alex cried, as if I'd met a celebrity.

"He made these crystals, so maybe there's a part of him in each of them," I said with a shrug. "And I'm sorry about scaring you and teleporting you all over."

"It's okay," Yancy said, finishing off his chicken. "It was terrifying, but it worked."

"So, should we stay here until dawn?" Destiny asked.

Alex peeked over the windowsill. "As long as no one bothers us, we stay here," she decided. "But just because they haven't found us yet doesn't mean they won't. We have to be on our guard."

"After all this excitement, I say we don't worry unless there's a reason to worry," Yancy said. "I was about to panic when Stevie went full-on Enderman. But you were right to trust him, Maison."

Maison smiled. "I know Stevie. We're best friends."

I smiled back her. But it felt dishonest. We almost hadn't been best friends. I had almost helped the Ender Dragon. If the Ender Dragon had *almost* gotten me to serve her once, she might actually succeed in the future.

"There was something else," I said. "I got the feeling that Endermen can only sense the general area around a crystal. I think the only reason I could sense that specific crystal was because it was already out of its hiding place and it was nearby. I couldn't sense any of the other crystals."

"That's too bad," Yancy said. "We could make you a crystal-sniffing Enderman, if you know what I mean."

I didn't, but I could tell Yancy thought he was being funny.

Alex rose up a little bit and peered out the window again. "Uh, guys?" she asked.

We all looked at her.

"It's time to start worrying," she said.

CHAPTER 19

WE ALL CLAMORED FOR OUR CHANCE TO LOOK out the window. The whole area in front of the shack was crowded with different mobs. First I saw armed skeletons, zombies, and giant spiders. There were also about a dozen Endermen. They had found us.

We all ducked down.

"What do we do?" I asked in a panicked whisper. I gripped the crystal shard close as if that would protect it.

"This house is only made of wood," Yancy said. "It's not going to give us much protection."

Just then something began banging on the wooden door. I could tell from the hisses and moans that it was a pack of zombies. That was the only door—we were trapped!

Alex ran to the other side of the shack. "Maybe we can break the window and get out that way!"

We all ran after her. But when we reached the window, we saw just as many zombies, skeletons, and giant spiders in the back. The only good news was that we didn't see any extra Endermen on this side of the shack.

The crystal throbbed in my hand and I heard the Ender Dragon's voice mocking me. *It's not too late to join my army,* she hissed. *I can protect you from all this.*

I gripped my head. When I wasn't in Enderman mode, her voice hurt so much!

"Stevie, what is it?" Maison asked frantically.

"We have to get out of here," I said. "It's hours until dawn. The house won't last that long."

Just as I said that, a block got dislodged from the wall. We all stared in horror. Now there was a hole in the wall, like a window but without a plane of glass. Through the hole I could see a giant Enderman holding the block it had taken from the house.

We had to come up with a plan, and quick! I wished Dad were here to help, or Steve Alexander. Why wouldn't Steve Alexander's voice come back now and tell me what to do?

The zombies pounded harder on the door. The mobs outside screeched and shrieked.

More blocks began disappearing from the wall. In

a matter of seconds, the Enderman would have cleared enough space to get in!

Suddenly I knew what to do. I turned to my friends and said, "I have to turn into an Enderman again."

CHAPTER 20

"STEVIE, ARE YOU CRAZY?" YANCY SAID. "WE barely got you back last time."

"But you can climb on my back and I can teleport with you!" I said. "We have to get away fast. If we can make it back to my home, we'll be safe. It has iron doors and a water block to protect it from mobs!"

The others looked around wildly. The Endermen were pulling out more blocks until there was a door-size hole in the wall.

The first Enderman came into the house, followed by two more.

I couldn't think of any other options. Even if I could, there wasn't time!

"Get ready!" I shouted, tossing the crystal shard to Maison. If I ran right into the Endermen with the shard, they might steal it and I wouldn't be able to transform back into myself.

Maison caught the crystal shard in her hands like a baseball. And I went charging toward the first Enderman, even though everything in me screamed not to. Yancy was right—it was crazy to run straight for a dangerous mob so I could turn into a dangerous mob myself!

Remember who you are! I thought as I ran. *This time, you can't let yourself be tempted by the Ender Dragon!*

I ran straight into an Enderman. Everything went dark and cold again. My body quickly grew taller. My mind clouded. I stepped back, blinking down at the kids by me. One of them was holding a crystal shard. I really wanted it.

"Stevie!" the girl shouted. "It's Maison. Take us home!"

Home! I almost wanted to shake my head to clear it. I didn't want to steal the crystal shard—I wanted to get home!

The kids all piled onto my back. I was distracted by the crystal again, but then another Enderman like me stepped up close, hissing in my face. That Enderman was mad because I had the crystal and wasn't sharing. I would show that Enderman!

I teleported outside the shack, right into the middle of a whole crowd of mobs. The zombies tried to grab me, and the skeletons pulled back their arrows. Before any of them could hurt me, I teleported again.

When I reappeared, the house was far behind me. The mobs were running after me, and the Endermen were teleporting my way. Even though I was so far ahead, more zombies and skeletons came out from behind the nearby trees and came after me.

Stevie, the voice called. It was not a good voice. So why did I want to listen to it?

Stevie, the voice called again in my head. *You don't have to fight me. We can be friends. Steve Alexander was a fool when he chose to fight against me instead of beside me. You don't want to make the same mistake, do you?*

I tried to ignore the voice, but it was really hard. Each time I teleported, I was surrounded by mobs again. Mostly they were zombies and skeletons, but a few times I appeared right next to a creeper. I had to teleport again extra fast to make sure the creeper didn't blow us all up!

This was a much longer distance than teleporting from the mountainside to the house. It was a good thing the others had all eaten some food right before this to get their strength up, because the more we teleported, the weaker they felt. I knew that each time we teleported between one spot and the next, they weren't able to breathe. It was like being underwater. So each time I reappeared, they all sucked in huge breaths.

Can your friends make it all the way to your home? the voice asked sweetly. She almost sounded like she was on my side. Like she was concerned about my friends. *You should stop where you are, Stevie. It will be better for them not to teleport anymore.*

Her comments got under my skin. I could tell my friends were really uncomfortable and I didn't want that. But I knew that if I stopped, it would be so much worse.

I know you have fought many mobs before, but I am different, the voice said. *I am misunderstood. Bring that crystal to the End with you and I will explain everything. You'll see.*

No! I shouted back in my mind. *There's a reason Steve Alexander locked you away! You want to destroy the Overworld!*

Lies! she said. *I've been so lonely trapped here. When I saw you and your friends during your brief visit to the End, it reminded me of the world outside. It showed me that it was possible to leave the End. I decided it was finally time to break free of this prison. And you will help me. You will* bow *to me!*

Never! I thought. But there was something dark and sinister growing in my head. The more the creepy voice talked, the more I liked it, even though I couldn't say why. Maybe she was telling the truth. Maybe Steve Alexander had lied in his book. He had said that he was foolish and full of himself, hadn't he? Maybe that meant he had been wrong to lock the Ender Dragon away.

I didn't hurt you when you came to the End before, she said. *What does that tell you?*

I didn't know. I felt so confused. I hadn't even known I was supposed to fight the Ender Dragon until this morning, and now her voice wouldn't get out of my head.

"Stevie!" Alex cried. "Stop!"

CHAPTER 21

FROZE. EVERYONE ON MY BACK WAS PANTING REALLY hard. Had I been teleporting too fast for them to catch their breath?

Zombies were emerging from behind the trees, staggering toward us.

"Grab some food," Yancy said. He handed everyone a bit of food from his backpack and they all shoved it in their mouths. I knew they desperately needed a break. We were about halfway back to my home. Would they make it?

The zombies were coming closer and closer. As soon as everyone got their bite of food down, Maison yelled, "Go!" and I disappeared again. We barely made it away before the zombies reached us.

Look at how they suffer, the Ender Dragon said. *Is this any way to treat friends? If you knew how Steve*

Alexander had treated me, you would think differently about him.

"Hurry, Stevie!" Maison said. "The other Endermen are still following us!"

I realized I was so caught up in what the Ender Dragon was saying that I'd stopped for a moment after reappearing. I glanced back. The same dozen Endermen were teleporting behind us, trying to catch up. I vanished again, trying to clear my head. I wished the Ender Dragon would leave me alone!

Maybe she was trying to confuse me and distract me on purpose. Since I couldn't talk, I couldn't even tell the others what was going on and ask them for help.

And the land out here was so dark, even though my Enderman eyes could see better in the dark than human eyes. We'd left the torch back at the shack in our hurry to get out, so we had no way to light our path. The way things were going, we'd be battling all night. And Endermen could survive in sunlight, so even the dawn wouldn't save us.

I pushed myself to teleport farther with each jump. It was hard, but it worked. And it didn't seem to affect the others any more than normal teleportation. But when I glanced behind me, I saw that all dozen Endermen were still following. I hadn't thrown them off my trail at all.

Then I finally saw a light in the distance. It was

the village near my home! After the next jump, I could make out some of the houses.

That was strange. There were a lot more torches than I remembered there being at night. And a lot of the villagers were out, even though it was after dark. In fact, it looked like lots of extra people, as if a few villages had all gathered.

At the edge of the village were a man and a woman, giving orders like they were leading an army. My heart leapt with hope.

It was Dad and Aunt Alexandra!

I teleported right to the edge of the village and stopped. Everyone slid off my back as Dad came running over. I was so glad to see him!

"We made it!" Maison said as she stood on wobbly feet.

"I think I need to sit down," Yancy wheezed.

But that's when Dad reached us. He lifted his diamond sword high in the air and swung it at me, shouting, "Begone, monster!"

CHAPTER 22

DAD'S DIAMOND SWORD CAME RUSHING AT ME and I had to teleport a few feet away to dodge it. I tried to yell to him that it was me, Stevie. But I still couldn't speak!

"Uncle Steve, no!" Alex shouted. "That's Stevie!"

Dad looked at me, his eyes wild in the torchlight. "Stevie?"

"Look at his eyes," Maison said. "When he transforms he gets an Enderman's height, but his eyes are the same!" She didn't wait for Dad to say anything. Instead, she ran over to me and touched my shoulder with the crystal shard.

There was a puff of purple light and then I was back to being myself.

"Stevie!" Dad exclaimed, kneeling beside me. "I

had no idea! I got your note. Your aunt and I got people from different villages together to help you!"

"This is the second crystal shard," Maison said.
"But the mobs are after it!"

Dad took a quick look at the approaching
Endermen, and the zombies and skeletons flanking
them. "Everyone get ready!" he shouted to the villagers. "Don't let them near the crystal!"

Aunt Alexandra fussed over Alex. "You look sick!"
she said.

"Just exhausted from teleporting," Alex said. Her
eyelids were drooping.

"Yeah, let's not do that again," Yancy said, pulling
more food out of his backpack. "Who's hungry?"

Alex, Maison, and Destiny dove for the food. Yancy
grabbed some for himself too, and they polished it all
off in seconds.

I turned my attention back to the approaching
mobs. With so many villagers around we might have a
chance of defeating them all, but it would still be hard.
I gripped my diamond sword, glad I hadn't lost it when
I was an Enderman and not thinking clearly.

An Enderman teleported right next to us, reaching for the crystal in Maison's hands. I lashed out
with my sword, driving the Enderman back. But a
moment later three more Endermen appeared, surrounding us.

Roaring, the villagers ran to battle. The ones near us were hitting at the Endermen with their own weapons. Others ran just outside of the village, where all the zombies and skeletons were. The air was thick with arrows from both villagers and skeletons.

I struck at the Endermen as they came close, but the battle was a blur. There were so many mobs pressed all around us! Every time I knocked one Enderman out of the way another came to replace it. They were so tall it was like they were blotting out part of the sky. I felt myself getting closed in. I missed how powerful I'd felt as an Enderman. But I was glad to have my own mind back.

Don't be so certain, Stevie.

That awful voice!

You could hear me when you found the first crystal, the voice said. *We were connected then. Since you became an Enderman, we're even more connected now. I know you better than you know yourself, Stevie. I know who Steve Alexander really* was. *And I know the true story of the Overworld's beginnings. You know nothing.*

I was so distracted by the voice that an Enderman was able to push right past me. It hurried toward Maison, reaching out to seize the crystal.

CHAPTER 23

"**N**O!" I SHOUTED. I SWUNG MY SWORD. THE ENderman disappeared to avoid being hit, so Maison and the crystal were safe for the moment. How was I going to fight if that voice kept talking to me?

The Ender Dragon must have known how distracting she was, because she kept speaking. *You can't get rid of me that easily,* the Ender Dragon hissed. *My power is only beginning to grow. At first only Endermen obeyed my wishes, but now other mobs are doing so as well. Before long I'll be out of the End myself, and there will be no way to defeat me.*

"Stevie, look out!" Maison called. She pushed me out of the way before a skeleton's arrow flew past, right where I'd been standing. Alex jumped over and shot the nearby skeleton with her own bow and arrow, taking it out for us.

Another Enderman came forward, and Dad struck it with his diamond sword, bellowing. Dad was on a rampage, hitting most of the mobs that tried to get close to us. But there were so many monsters that a few still got through.

"Take out the Endermen first!" I heard Aunt Alexander shout. "The Endermen are leading the charge!"

Everyone turned their attention on the Endermen. Arrows flew. Swords slashed. In a matter of seconds, the twelve Endermen were gone.

The other mobs got a little less frenzied for a second. It was like they weren't sure what to do.

It didn't take them long to figure that out, though. A hostile mob is a hostile mob. Maybe they weren't as smart as the Endermen, but they knew to attack people. As I watched, more and more mobs were marching out of the darkness and toward the village. There were monsters almost as far as I could see.

CHAPTER 24

"WE HAVE TO GET BACK HOME," I SAID. "WE can hide the crystal there, and they won't be able to get inside. We can wait until dawn!"

Dad shouted, "Villagers! A few of us will take the crystal someplace safer. The mobs should follow us there."

"How do you know the mobs will follow you?" one villager demanded angrily. He had a diamond sword that he was using to defend his home. "You might just be leaving us alone against them all!"

Dad shook his head. "Watch. Kids, Alexandra, come with me!"

We did. As soon as we started running out of the village with Dad and Aunt Alexandra, everything changed. The mobs stopped going after the other people at the village and came after us instead. The angry man was gaping as zombies walked past him as if he wasn't even there.

We all stayed together as a group to make it harder for the mobs to hit us. But we were still being attacked by something with almost every step. And more mobs were constantly at our heels.

"Creeper!" I shouted, noticing one right ahead. It started to shake, getting ready to explode, but Alex got it with her arrow first. The creeper vanished, and I felt a moment of relief. That moment didn't last very long.

If only I could turn into an Enderman again! That would let us move so much faster. But there weren't any more Endermen around and . . .

And you won't be able to resist me for long, the Ender Dragon said. *You thought you were getting a handle on things, but it was only temporary. The more times you turn into an Enderman, the better my spirit will be able to possess you.*

No! I thought. If it was that big of a risk, I'd never turn into an Enderman again!

The Ender Dragon sniffed. *It doesn't matter to me,* she said. *I will have you one way or another.*

"The mobs are everywhere!" Yancy cried, pushing back a zombie that had staggered up to him. More zombies were right behind it.

Dad let out a low growl as his sword slashed through

the horde of mobs. "You kids stay close to me," he said. "We're going to make it!"

I wasn't so sure.

Stevieee, the voice called. It was singsongy, in a mocking, cruel way.

Leave me alone! I thought back at the voice.

I have a surprise for you, she said.

She was right. When our house came in view, we saw the entire place was surrounded by mobs.

And all of them were ready to attack.

CHAPTER 25

DAD FROZE. I WAITED FOR HIM TO TELL US WHAT to do or say something encouraging.

Instead, he said, "There's no way we can reach the house."

"No!" It took me a moment to realize I'd shouted that. In my head, the Ender Dragon let out a low snicker.

The mobs were mostly zombies, but I also saw an Enderman in the crowd, standing at the front of the pack like a guard. As soon as the mobs saw us, they began heading our way.

What do we do? I thought frantically. There was no way to plow through all these mobs—even Dad thought so!

Then I had an idea.

I could turn into an Enderman again. Everyone

could grab on and I could teleport us all right in front of the door. Once we were in the house, the Enderman wouldn't be able to get in because of the water, and the zombies wouldn't be able to get past the iron door. We would be able to just wait until dawn, when most of the mobs would be gone.

It would only take one quick teleportation. I'd resisted the Ender Dragon before. But was it too risky? What did she mean when she said, *The more you turn into an Enderman, the better my spirit will be able to possess you*?

"I have to do this," I said. "Everyone, as soon as I'm done, take out the other Enderman and hop on my back!"

Just like before, I ran at the Enderman before anyone could try to talk me out of it. I heard Dad, Aunt Alexandra, and Maison all shouting something, but I couldn't make it out over the hissing of the zombies.

Remember who you are the whole time, Stevie! I ordered myself as I leapt at the Enderman.

I felt the blackness and the cold again. It was even worse than I remembered. I felt myself grow. I stood there blinking down from my height, half aware as someone behind me shot the other Enderman through with arrows. I felt as if I should care about what happened to my fellow Enderman, but I didn't. There was only one being I really cared about.

Welcome back, Stevie, the Ender Dragon said.

Yes, my queen, I responded.

CHAPTER 26

I TURNED ON THE HUMANS BEHIND ME AND WATCHED them all shrink back in fear. The girl was holding the crystal shard. The crystal shard that belonged to my queen!

I lunged for her. She cried out and took a step back. Zombies were coming up from behind me to help in my mission, and even more approached the people from behind. There was no way they could escape.

"Stevie!" a man yelled at me. "I'm your father. Take us to the door!"

Why would I listen to him?

Take the crystal from the Earth girl and teleport directly to the End, the Ender Dragon said. *Then you will be given a reward.*

It's enough just to serve you, my queen, I thought.

Even though I couldn't see her face, the sound of her voice made me think she was smiling. *Excellent.*

"Not this again!" said the boy. "Stevie, it's Yancy! Stop scaring us and remember who you are."

What was there to remember? I knew who I was. I was the Enderman Stevie, the servant of the Queen Ender Dragon. That's who I'd always been.

"You chose to turn into an Enderman to protect us!" the girl with the crystal said. "Remember us? Your friends and family? We built a tree house together! We've gone on so many adventures!"

That sounded vaguely familiar. But the mobs were really closing in on them. Maybe if I just sat this out, the mobs would take care of the kids and the crystal shard would be mine. I wouldn't even have to do extra work for it.

No, the Ender Dragon scolded. *Take it from her. Don't be lazy, my Stevie. Destroy the girl who holds my crystal. If you love me, you'll do this.*

I did love my queen. I stepped up to the girl. I would destroy her and take her crystal.

She let out a scream and struck out at me with her weapon, knocking me back. For some reason, that scream made me pause. Something deep inside of me wanted to help someone who screamed like that. I could tell they were scared. Why would I attack someone who was that scared?

So what if she's scared? the Ender Dragon said. *That just makes her easier to defeat. Take what's ours.*

Suddenly, I knew what I had to do.

CHAPTER 27

THE ENDER DRAGON SAW MY RESPONSE AND BE-
gan to roar in fury. *No!* she shrieked. *Nooo!*

I'd turned and gestured for my friends to jump on my back. They all did, and as soon as they were holding on, I teleported us directly in front of the house, being careful not to get water on myself.

I will still have you! the Ender Dragon rampaged. *You have no chance of collecting all the crystal shards! And when I'm free from the End, I will go after you first!*

Everything happened in a flash. The people jumped off my back, Aunt Alexandra hit the switch to open the door, and Dad fought back the mobs all trying to converge on us. In a rush, I remembered who these people were—they were the most important people in the Overworld to me. Maison touched me on the shoulder with the crystal and I was back to being myself.

"Get inside!" Aunt Alexandra cried as the door opened. We all rushed in so fast we got wedged in the doorway for a second. Then we all flew through. Zombies were trying to push their way in behind us, but Dad shoved them backward with his sword and closed the door. The zombies kept hissing and spitting and clawing at the door, but we knew they couldn't get in now.

"Stevie, what happened there?" Dad exclaimed.

I realized I was shaking. "The Ender Dragon keeps talking to me! She says she's the one who's right, and Steve Alexander is wrong, and I have to listen to her!"

Dad gave me a hug. For a moment, I was surprised—Dad wasn't much of a hugger. It almost seemed like he was trying to prove to himself that I was still there and in one piece.

"But you resisted her," Dad said. "I used the first crystal earlier to read what Steve Alexander said in the book. That's why I got all the villagers together. The Ender Dragon is much stronger than any mob in the Overworld—much stronger than Herobrine ever was. It will take everything we have to defeat her."

"D-do you think we *can* defeat her?" I stammered. I wasn't feeling so sure.

"With the Overworld Heroes task force and all the people of the Overworld behind us, yes," Aunt Alexandra said in a strong voice. "I think we can."

"I kept losing myself and then coming back," I said.

"I don't understand it. There was always something reminding me of who I was when I was an Enderman."

"It was your humanity," Aunt Alexandra said. "You have to be strong in the face of evil like this."

I looked at Dad. "I'm sorry we ran off earlier," I said. "We didn't know what to do."

"I wasn't happy about it, but I understand," Dad said. "After reading that book, I knew I needed to act immediately, too."

"Hey," Maison said. "Let's see if the second crystal lets us read more!"

We all looked at one another, then ran to get the book.

CHAPTER 28

ESTINY LOWERED THE SECOND CRYSTAL OVER the part of the book where the first crystal had stopped being able to translate it for us. Under the new crystal, the gibberish turned to real worlds.

"*If you are reading this,*" Destiny read aloud, "*then you have found the second crystal. I must make the path to finding the crystals difficult because it also helps ensure that the Ender Dragon doesn't find them first. Be warned that she is tricky. She will try to convince you to side with her.*"

I shivered. He was right about that! Did that mean the Ender Dragon had tried to get Steve Alexander on her side too? But everything she said was a lie—wasn't it?

"*If you are brave and strong, you can find the other crystals,*" Destiny continued to read. "*And know that even if I am not there with you in person, I am there with you in spirit during your journey."*

I shivered again. But this time it was a shiver of amazement. Did what Steve Alexander had written mean that it was his voice I'd heard earlier? That voice had saved me. Thinking about it now also made me feel a little stronger.

"Is he going to go into his life story again?" Yancy asked.

"No. There's another map," Destiny said, moving the crystal over it. "This must be where we have to go next."

We all bent over the book.

"It's a jungle," Dad said. "I've never been there before."

"Then that's where we'll go next," Alex said.

"First, you kids need to get some rest," Aunt Alexandra said, sounding more like a mom than the mayor who made us into a task force. "In the morning most of the mobs will be gone. We can discuss what to do next then."

Part of me felt too wound up for sleep. But another part of me was exhausted. Dad and Aunt Alexandra made some beds for Maison, Destiny, and Yancy to sleep over, and Alex took the guest bedroom. I got ready to lie down in my own comfy, safe bed with my cat Ossie. I could hardly believe everything that had happened.

I could still hear zombies crying out in the night, but we were secure inside. I had overcome the Ender Dragon's attempts to control me, even though there had been a few close calls. And I could almost feel the strength of my ancestor Steve Alexander pumping through my veins. He was going to be with me, along with my family and my task force—I mean, my friends.

I will never bow to you, I told the Ender Dragon. And then I went to sleep.

WANT MORE OF STEVIE AND HIS FRIENDS?

Read the Unofficial Overworld Adventure series!

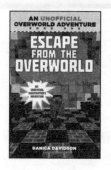

Escape from the Overworld
DANICA DAVIDSON

Attack on the Overworld
DANICA DAVIDSON

The Rise of Herobrine
DANICA DAVIDSON

Down into the Nether
DANICA DAVIDSON

The Armies of Herobrine
DANICA DAVIDSON

Battle with the Wither
DANICA DAVIDSON

Available wherever books are sold!

DO YOU LIKE FICTION FOR MINECRAFTERS?

Read the
Unofficial Minecrafters Academy series!

Zombie Invasion
WINTER MORGAN

Skeleton Battle
WINTER MORGAN

Battle in the Overworld
WINTER MORGAN

Attack on Minecrafters Academy
WINTER MORGAN

Hidden in the Chest
WINTER MORGAN

Encounters in End City
WINTER MORGAN

DO YOU LIKE FICTION FOR MINECRAFTERS?

You'll Love Books for Terrarians!

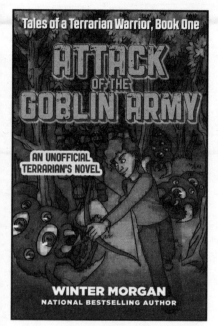

Attack of the Goblin Army
Winter Morgan

Snow Fight
Winter Morgan

Welcome to Terraria, a land of adventure and mystery. Build a shelter, craft weapons to battle bosses, explore the biomes, collect coins and gems . . .

Join Miles and his friends on amazing adventures in

The Tales of a Terrarian Warrior series!

Available wherever books are sold!